# (LIFE Through Hers.)

When Life Happens Right Before Your Eyes!

## Written by: Jannette Lane-Peterkin

# ALMOND EYES (LIFE Through Hers!)

## Written by: Jannette Lane-Peterkin

## Cover Art: Jasmine Rebecca Peterkin

**ISBN:** 9798445752899
**Imprint:** Independently published

All Scripture quotations are taken from the King James Bible.

# ACKNOWLEDGEMENTS

I would like to thank God Almighty for the gifts that he has given me. I would like to thank you, Jesus, for salvation. Thank you to the Holy Spirit for being my guide.

I would like to thank my husband, children, grandchildren, and my mother for their inspiration and support. Thanks to all of my prayer partners for keeping me lifted up in much prayer. May the Peace and Blessings of God be with you all!

# TABLE OF CONTENTS

1. Chapter 1: A Beautiful Beginning (page 5)

2. Chapter 2: Vanilla (page 29)

3. Chapter 3: HOME (page 42)

# Chapter 1

## (A Beautiful Beginning)

It was a beautiful beginning of a Spring morning. Stacia had just arrived at her bakery, 'Sweet Peaces of Treats'. It was all she could do to contain herself as she walked up to the front door. There she stood looking at the bright red neon sign. "Peace Treats!" Mine, all mine!" It had been a life-long dream of Stacia's to own her very own bakery, especially, after working in one for the last four years. And Stacia always loved baking, as she remembered her mother showing her how to make Mom's vanilla walnut cake.

Stacia was forty-six, married with three children. Kayla was twenty-two, Niguel was seventeen, and Libby was fifteen. But, even after giving birth to three children, Stacia had reverted to her high school figure. She was about five feet, six inches tall, one hundred and forty-eight pounds. Her hair was dark brown, shoulder length, very thick and bouncy. Her skin was a mix of caramel with a hint of light copper. But the one thing that stood out the most on Stacia, and she received many compliments for, were her beautiful, brown almond-shaped eyes. These eyes made her look exotic. They always appeared slightly closed as if the sun were shining in her eyes. Stacia was also a born-again believer, which required her to live a modest life. She was very serious about her calling as a teacher of God's word. And she worked hard as a Kingdom woman

Stacia had been married to her husband Gabriel, for fourteen years now. But, all of the drama the last seven years, made it seem like forever. There were many good days in their marriage. That is the earlier times. But as time progresses people change. Some change for the better and some simply get worse. Gabriel had chosen the backsliding path of worse. Gabriel owned his own recycling company for the last three years. He was also a minister at his church. But, unlike Stacia, he didn't take his calling very serious at all. He spent much of his time chasing money, fame, and now women. Praying, fasting, caring for the church was very last on his list, almost non-existent. In seven years, he had transformed into a whole other man. A stranger who Stacia was beginning to dislike. His family was also becoming less of a priority.

Stacia kept the books and managed the office. That is, up until the recent year, when she decided that she was consumed by her husband's dream and losing sight of her own. The world was changing rapidly, and anything could happen at any time. And more importantly, God could call them home at any time, and Stacia would not have fulfilled her life's dream. Let's just say it was not all roses in the Caswell house.

"Naa na, naa na, naa, na na!" She danced her way into the door. "Great morning!" Stacia greeted her two employees. "How's everybody doing today?" she asked. "Well..., what you want me to start with, humph? My broken nail. Or my hurting foot. Which is mainly hurting because you made me work all.... day yesterday. When I told you that my bunion was bothering me!" said Tanya. "I mean, what kind of boss are you anyway? I've been wondering that deez days." she smirked as she smacked her lips. And they were very full lips, covered in candy apple red lip gloss. That's Tanya, as some would call her 'Miss Country Bama Bougie'. She made decent money, that she would spend luxuriously at the flea market. Like, on those lime green wedges that she wears every second Friday, with her pineapple- print bell bottoms.

Stacia inquisitively asked Tanya, "Why do you switch-talk like that, when you graduated as double major, on the president's list, and worked in the business district for the last decade?" "What you mean? This is how I grew up in the country. You see, my nana used to dip snuff. So, she never pronounced words right because her mouth was always full. But I didn't care about none of that. I thought my nana was the funniest person in the world, and I loved her dearly. I said when I grow up, I wanna talk just like my nana, just without the snuff. I don't want no brown teeth. I love to look good, you know!" said Tanya as she strolled back and forth striking a pose. Angela responded saying, "So, your nana spoke country hood too. You feel me? That's what she said. Because I'm pretty sure that saying wasn't even out while she was living!" "Watch yo' mouth when talking about my nana!" exclaimed Tanya as she pretended to slap Angela. "No, the hood slang came from my old Boo Tony. He was from the hood section of the Bayou. They got gangster over there. He taught me a little pillow talk that's all," answered Tanya as she looked at Stacia's unapproving look at how the conversation was going south. "I mean, that is before I came to the Lord. We ain't always been saved now. Bump, bump!" Tanya yelled as she danced around Stacia. "And besides I'm not ashamed of being Black. Some of us speak different dialect sometimes, but that don't mean we're stupid. Shoot, My Uncle Percy never went to college and he's a millionaire. He had a genius mind when he made those coffee lids for Bros. To Go Cups." Tanya said as she fluffed her braids into Angela's face. Angela pushed Tanya out of the way and

said "Yeah, Yeah, we know!"
"Noted. I'm not saying it's a bad
thing. Just wondering how you
flow, Sis." Stacia said with a
smile.

"Tanya, did you forget to bring
the donuts again?" Angela
whined. "Oops, my bad!" laughed
Tanya. She whispered to Stacia,
"A donut is the last thing that she
needs. She is one sprinkle away,
from her big tail being hoisted
out of here with a crane!" Stacia
popped Tanya on the arm,
shushing her up. "Oh, you know
you were thinking it!" retorted
Tanya. "Here you go, Angela. I got
the Donuts today. And it's some
of those chocolate ones with the
sprinkles on them, just like you
like them. Of course, you know,

Tanya, can be a bit testy about this time of the month." tooted Stacia. "Oh no. Is this the anniversary day again?" Angela asked with a mouthful of doughnut. "Exactly!" Stacia responded. "Yes. It's the day that Mark CHEATED on her, allegedly." "Oh...ungh,..un! don't even say allegedly. Because I caught the dog in the act. He was over there on Fifth Screet., when I told him that I did not want to see him on that street again. Especially, since that big-behind Ginger lives over there!" yelled Tanya. "So again, tell me how that constitutes as cheating, all because he was on Fifth Street.? And please explain it to me as if I'm in preschool. Because I still don't get it.  If you didn't see him doing anything, how was he cheating?" Stacia asked with a grin. Angela stood there nibbling her donut, while cutting her eyes at Stacia. She too was waiting to hear this. "Oh, naïve one. You've been married too long to know what it's like out here. Well, you just take a seat right there and let me tell you something. Let me school you's both on the actual, factual laws of love and obedience according to ME! It's like this, if Tanya has an enemy, then he has an enemy, so therefore WE... have an enemy! You feel me?" said Tanya. "And enlighten us again, to why she is your enemy? "Wow!" sighed Tanya. Here we go with the amnesia! Do you remember when we were in the eleventh grade, and I had that boyfriend named Sam? Well, did you see how Sam ended up in the back seat of his Mustang with Ginger? There she was, with her raggedy 'ole top down 'round her waist, and his hands in a place that they should never have touched!" squealed Tanya with a serious looks on her face as she squished a paper cup in her hand.

"Ha, ha, haagh... Stacia and Angela laughed, as they gave each other high five. "Every time you tell that story, the facts seem to change. I thought she had her shirt up over her head?" joked Angela. "Do you understand that you are about 40 years old now? It is time to let that go," scolded Stacia. "Oh, but no, see! Ya'll wanna make a mockery of my pain? No matter whether it was a long time or not, it was very painful and traumatic," Tanya said with dramatical tone. "You just don't understand. How could you? After all, you have the perfect marriage." She said with a crackling voice. Stacia sighed and said, "Well...., I wouldn't go that far." "Hol' up, hol' up! Wait a minute. What you mean? Is there trouble in paradise?" Tanya asked inquisitively. Stacia hesitantly responded, "Well... It ain't been paradise for a long time now." "What's going on?" both Tanya and Angela jumped up and pulled up a seat right in front of Stacia's desk.

They had all settled in the small front room that Stacia called her office. It was tiny but very comfortable. Stacia believed that work should be something that she loved, and she made her office a work oasis. The walls were pearl white, trimmed in beautifully stained oakwood. She had an Italian marble-topped desk, with a baby blue cushiony recliner office chair. There were pictures of her three children, and a very old picture of her and her husband Gabriel on the desk.

"Yeesh! Ya'll are so nosy. Is my life that interesting to you?" Stacia asked with her hands raised in the air. "Yes!" both Angela and Tanya responded with a quickness. Tanya added, "Yes, oh yes Punkin. Because, you never seem to have any problems." Angela shook her head and said, "That's right." "Well excuse me if I don't come in here and tell everybody, every terrible thing that happens to me, as if you can do something about it." "Well, you should. We're your sistas, and we got your back." said Tanya excitedly. Angela shook her head in agreement saying to Stacia "So, spill the tea girl!" "I don't know what to say. I mean...I... I just feel like I don't want to be married to him anymore. Stacia said resistantly. Tanya and Angela stood up immediately. Their smiles turned to faces of confused pain. They had never heard Stacia say anything about her marriage with such seriousness. "Hold on, you... Now, is it that you don't want to be married to him, or not married to anyone?  Just not married?" asked Angela as she wiped donut crumbs off her shirt. "What he did? That fool cheated, didn't he? I knew it, I knew it! I said it and I'll say it again.  All men cheat eventually!" yelled Tanya. Stacia raised her finger up as she tried to interject. Tanya quickly mouthed, "Uggh ungh, nopety, no! I know what you gonna say preacher lady. 'That's like saying that God can't keep anybody," Angela nodded in agreement with her eyes closed, as she snickered at Tanya mocking Stacia's voice. "Check it! I am the wise woman in here today," Tanya laughed a little. "I have found that every man is a dog about now! You turn yo' head for one dang second and he is looking at every thang with a heartbeat. I do mean thang," said Tanya dramatically as she wiggled her behind. Angela said, "I must agree with that. The only good men left that I know are my three nephews. And they are three, four, and six years old. And that six-year-old is hanging on by a tight thread. If he sees one more cartoon with the little sponge girl in her undies, it's all over for him!" "Oooh! See, you see, even the library lady done been cheated on!" said Tanya pointing to Angela. Stacia laughed silently. Angela looked at Tanya rolling her eyes, and said, "You got one more time, Evilina!"

"Well, you look like an old library lady, from the fifth grade, with that button up sweater, with dat butterfly collar," Tanya said jokingly. "Excuse me, 'Clueless in Melan Town'. This is a vintage look, which cost me one hundred and twenty-six dollars." Angela swooped her sweater across Tanya's head. Tanya swung the sweater off her head, while answering Angela, "That is called a very old, cruddy-sweater! Okay..." "Hey, Hey... Stacia laughed as she stood between Angela and Tanya as they play-boxed each other. I thought this was about me for a change.

You right said Tanya, let's get back to the cheater in yo' house!" "Look, I never said he cheated.

Well, I've never caught him cheating. There have been a few women that called his phone, but they said that it was a mistake when they heard my voice. One even said that it was 'ministry work'. I brushed those off." replied Stacia. Tanya and Angela stood with their mouths open wide. "And why didn't you tell us"? asked Tanya. "Because I knew that you would react just like you are now, very loudly and animated," said Stacia. What else has that ole' dog been up to?" Asked Tanya. "Well, it's not that. It's the lies mostly. I caught him in so many lies. And the porn, is just..." Stacia partially responded before she was cut off in mid-sentence. "Oh!... See, I told you Angela. Those preachers always love those freaky-videos. They try to come as close as they can to touching the boot-ay, without touching it!" exclaimed Tanya. "They think they slick. But you ain't ne'er fooled me with ya brown Sunday suit, and you brown Nicky Achin's shoes on. "Mggh-mggh-mggh!" said Tayna while shaking her head in disapproval. Tanya, I must say that you did say it girl" retorted Angela. "First, good Christian women don't talk like that. And have you two have been gossiping about me?" Stacia asked with a slight grin on her face. Tanya said, "Yeah, chic. You ain't exempt from being yapped on. Go on with the rest of it."

"It's just that the demons that he is playing with are taking over and he's become delusional." Responded Stacia. "Like the other night he was in the bed moving as if he were having sex with someone, but there was no one there. And it sure wasn't me, since this mess started, I have lost all desire for him." Tanya and Angela jumped back as if they saw a ghost. Angela said, "This is much deeper than we thought!" Stacia shook her head and said "Yeah. He is starting to say there's nothing wrong with women wearing short-shorts or super short mini-skirts. He will watch TV shows with inappropriate scenes and cursing, like it's nothing wrong with a minister doing these things. If you tell him what the bible says about the situation, he gets smoking angry. And then he'll tell you that the bible says all things are lawful, but everything may not be good for you." "What kind of snake foolishness is that? And what that mean anyway Teacher, all things are lawful?" Tanya asked with a scowl. Stacia responded, "He's taking the word of God and trying to justify his messed-up state. When the bible says in **1 Corinthians 10:23- All things are lawful for me, but all things are not expedient: all things are lawful for me, but all things edify not.** That means although you may be able to do something, it does not mean that it is good for you." "Now, even I know that the bible says, that if a man look at a woman to lust for her that he done already committed adultery in his heart. I may not have perfect attendance at church, but I know that one." Tanya said with a wrinkle in her forehead. "And the bible said we women, should dress in modest apparel not calling attention to OURSELVES, Tanya!" Angela said as she slid her glasses down to the point of her nose looking at Tanya's snug-fitting bell bottom pants. Tanya gave a deep squeal of a sigh as she prepared to respond to Angela's statement about her, but Stacia interrupted her. "Ladies, Ladies let's get to work. It's six-fifteen already and we have yet to shape the donuts." Stacia said as she clapped her hands together and guided each of the women to their stations. "Doors are always open at seven am for the early birds. Ya'll know this!" said Stacia. "Okay, but we goin' finish this later, because I got some solutions for you. He don't do my sista like that!" yelled Tanya. Angela gave Tanya the look of stop with the dramatics.

# Chapter 2

## (Vanilla)

They proceeded to get the cake, cookie, pie, and donut mixes together. They were all made with love and care. After all this was not just a business for Stacia. Baking was a favorite part of her life since a young girl. They had a menu with six donut flavors, mini pies, cupcakes, and full layer cakes. The sweet smell of vanilla and almond always filled the building. The walls were a pretty mix of yellow trimmed in blue and pink. The columns were designed with sprinkle images up and down the sides. The display cases were front and center with just enough light from the sun to illuminate the deliciously looking treats. There were four booths and four tables in the dining area. Stacia was not a big fan of people eating in, because that meant more germs and mess to clean up. Not everyone was as tidy as they were. In fact, some people could get scuzzy when it came to them leaving their trash and crumbs everywhere, but the trash can.

Stacia was the star of everything cakes and cupcakes. She knew how to make the most delicious cakes, even in the short amount of time. Every time she made her bestseller cake, the Thrilla Vanilla Mound cake, she would say, "God sure'nuff gave me the skills to pay the bills!"

The donuts were the fluffiest and most popular around Melan Town. Tanya was the queen of the donut. She was in charge of the donuts, mixing and shaping. She had a secret technique for making the melt in your mouth donuts. Her most popular creation was the Strawberry Sunshine. It was glazed with sweet strawberry drizzle, topped with moist pieces of lemon crumbs lined up in the form of sun rays. Stacia and Angela had yet to find out the recipe.

Angela was in charge of making the pies and cookies. You know that the star of her show was the sweet potato pie and her double chip, chocolate chip cookies. That pie was the slap-yo-momma good kind of pie. Stacia thought the secret lied in her butter and nutmeg combination. But it too was a secret. The Peace Treats bakery was full of heavenly surprises.

It was about closing time. The lunch flow had been really heavy. The ladies were whipped. Tanya plopped in her bean bag chair, took a deep sigh and said, "The countdown begins. In ten more minutes, it'll be five-thirty. I am locking that door at five twenty-five!" "Tanya, we close at five-thirty on the dot. You know Mrs. Neville has to get in here in the last five minutes to get cupcakes for her kids," said Stacia as she sweeps the dining room floor. "I got to get home. My show is coming on tonight, and I want to get me some 'Snickin Lickin Chickin' before I go home. Ain't nobody got time to be waiting to give some cupcakes to some little waterhead kids. Them kids got some big 'ole heads on them. Ya'll know I'm telling the truth!" exclaimed Tanya.

Angela added "Yeah! Stacia. I got to get home tonight. I got a date!" Stacia responded, "Really, that's great! Anyone we know?" Tanya said with a snicker, "Yeah. I think it's my sixty-seven year old

History professor from the university. Ha...ha...haagh!" "Shut it, Tanya!" shouted Angela. "He happens to be the Bible study teacher at my church. And he's single, kind, and saved. He's just what I asked God for." Good for you Angela. Love is real, and there are some good men out there. Despite what Tanya says. So, why don't you get going, so you can get ready for your date. Me and T. can finish up here," said Stacia with a smile. Tanya jokingly said to Angela, "Yes, Honey! You need some extra time to get ready. What you goin' do with dat Jherry curl? Drip, drip! I thought they went out of style in the late 80's!" She said this because Angela had naturally curly hair. She was part Black and part Puerto Rican. "You should know! It's the same time that those gold caps went right behind them!" Angela exclaimed licking her teeth as she walked out the door. "I'll get you tomorrow you hussy!" Tanya laughed as she swiped Angela across the back. Stacia shook her head saying "Have a blessed date, Ang."

"Five-thirty!" yelled Tanya. As Stacia stood looking out of the window, she said with a concerned expression on her face, "I wonder what happened to Mrs. Neville? She's always here on Thursdays for the donuts after hour sale." "Maybe one of those kids got their monkey-ball heads stuck in the fence post again,"

Tanya said with a giggle. "Tanya, quit it! You something else! You even got me talking like you now," Stacia shook her head in laughter. "Let's hit it, Sis.!" ordered Stacia, as they started cleaning out the display case.

It was six pm exactly when they locked the bakery doors, heading to their cars. Tanya drove a black Lane Hover with tinted windows and lived in a beautiful town house in the swanky part of Melan Town. It was souped up to the max with rims and all kinds of lights. Be not confused. Although Tanya spoke perfect Ebonics, she was a college graduate with a degree in Journalism. She was a sort of speech chameleon. She knew when to speak business and when to relax. After all, she was the head editor of the Zassy Magazine. Tanya ended up working at Peace Treats after she got fired for cursing out her boss, Michael. She said that he all but called her a racial slur, because she wouldn't go out with him. But Stacia and Angela always thought that there was more to the story.

Angela drove the sensible Shevy Swark to work. But she also owned a Paserati. See Angela was single and had received a very hefty inheritance from her grandparents who raised her. Angela's mother and father were both killed in a car accident when she was just four years old. Both her grandparents had passed away from natural causes one year apart. She didn't have to work at the bakery at all. She was also a college graduate with a degree in Psychology. But she just didn't have the heart to go back to work at her medical facility, Calmer Waters, after her grandmother died. So, she started working at the bakery with Stacia and Tanya. And Stacia couldn't be happier that they were both there. Especially since these were her two closest friends from grade school.

Stacia drove a cobalt blue Lane Cruiser and a pearl color Baudi, but not to work. She would always drive the bakery van to work as a form of advertisement.

And she also didn't see the sense in drawing attention to herself, especially since the bakery was in the city area, where crime was picking up rather quickly.

"Stacia, why you drive that pastry van to work when you got those two nice rides. Girl, you see how I roll! Aye!" said Tanya as she danced around. Stacia responded, "It's called advertisement! And besides, the bible says know the times and seasons that we are living in. You know Donna from the Pharmacy right down the street got carjacked two weeks ago. It's a blessing that she is still alive. Because they don't just take your car anymore, they kill now." "The devil is a liar! I wish some fool would roll up on me and try to take my Hover, that I done worked so hard to get. I had to put up with some stank breath e'ery day for this ride. And you know what I mean!" exclaimed Tanya. Stacia side eyed her and said, "Tanya, you better not try to fight somebody over a jeep that you have insured and can replace. You can't replace you!" "Sis, I ain't got to fight nobody. I got a showstopper for every criminal who's trying to get in the spotlight," replied Tanya as she pulled a shiny silver nine-millimeter gun out of her purse. "Put that down. What is that? What are you doing with that?" Stacia asked with urgency. "What! You just said that the bible said know what time it is.

And God didn't say you can't have a weapon," said Tanya. "Ooh! I... We will talk about this tomorrow. And you better not bring that thing into my bakery. I mean it Tanya! exclaimed Stacia with a serious look. "What!" responded Tanya. "Later Tanya. I'll see you tomorrow, God's will. And put that thing up before you shoot somebody, shoot yourself, or somebody shoots you. And don't get pulled over by the cops, because that's a whole other ball game," commanded Stacia. Tanya jokingly said, "Later Mommy!" They both drove off to their homes.

# Chapter 3

## (Home)

Just as Stacia pulled into her driveway, she started to get those knots in her stomach, just thinking about what the complaint was going to be tonight. Lately, all Gabriel did, was complain about what he does not have, and what he's not getting enough of, or what he doesn't like. Stacia was at the breaking point when it came to even conversating with him at all.

As she exited the van, she was greeted by her pet German Shephard, Sam. He was a beautiful brown and black colored Shep. He was also most loyal to Stacia than anyone else in the family since she treated him like he was one of her children. "Hey, buddy! She said as Sam jumped on her gently. She had trained him not to be too rough, as he was easy to train.

She was greeted at the door by her son Niguel. He was momma's boy all the way. He was also her only son. "Hello there Momma!" he said as he took the box of doughnuts from her hands. Stacia stood with one hand on her hip and said, "That's what it's all about? Some doughnuts? Hey to you too apple headed boy!" She called him that because he of his big funny shaped head. Once when she was out to eat with Gabriel and Niguel, an elderly Chinese woman had said to them, that the way the baby's head was shaped told her that he was going to be very smart. And he was intelligent for sure. He skipped a grade, going into college early and landing on the dean's list. He was studying to be an engineer. "Where's Libby?" Stacia asked. "Here I am Ma!" Libby responded as she skipped towards Stacia. "Hey, Lady! Did you clean that kitchen, like I told you?" Stacia asked her sternly. Libby was pretty much all over the place. She was still in High School, quite smart, pretty like mom with one dimple on her right cheek. When she was born, the head nursery nurse called the dimple a stork's bite. The pediatric doctor even told Stacia that Libby had a very special personality. And that she did, as she was a little bossy, but comical kid. Libby and Niguel were very close since they were so close in age.

Gabriel came in the house twenty minutes later after working at the recycling company all day, Stacia supposed. He always threw his dirty gloves and jacket on the front room floor, which peeved Stacia so bad. "Gabriel don't put those germy close on the floor in the living room. Take those things to the bin at the back hallway. Why don't you just leave them in the garage?" Stacia questioned with an aggravated tone. "Woman, leave me alone. This is my house, and I can do what I want!" said Gabriel with his lips stuck out for a kiss. It took everything in Stacia not to take off running, but she braced herself and kissed him. Immediately afterwards she wiped her lips with the wet cloth that she kept in her apron pocket. Stacia no longer trusted Gabriel because of his shifty behavior lately. After all, she didn't know where his lips had been.

"What's for dinner Baby?" Gabriel asked as he washed his filthy hands in the kitchen sink. "There he goes again, Mr. Nasty," whispered Libby to herself. "I heard that. Hush it up!" Stacia said pointing at Libby. Libby responded with a sneaky grin, "Did I say that out loud?" Stacia gave her a side eye look. Although Libby had just revealed how Stacia really felt. She was just fed up with him and his whole act. "Tonight's the night. I have to tell him," Stacia said to herself. "We're having baked chicken casserole man!" she responded to Gabriel.

Stacia and Gabriel always sat together watching funny sitcoms while they ate dinner. The kids would watch their own shows together. But, on Sundays they all ate together as a family tradition. It was supposed to keep the family talking, which was said to help keep things together. But whoever wrote that saying, just didn't know any better. Because they left the key ingredient out of that Sunday togetherness recipe. That is God!

It used to be a highlight of the day, when she looked forward to eating dinner with her man. She would laugh so hard at his animated jokes. He would look with pride as his wife loved on him that way. But, how the tide had turned. Now, she could barely stand to look at him. The sight of him chewing just made her nauseous. He had gone from sweet, humble, and charming; into a greedy, disrespectful, jabber-jaw creep. When times were sweeter and their love was stronger, she used to think that everything he did was the cutest. But now everything he did made her boil with disgust. "Oh, My Gosh! Look at him chewing that food with his mouth all open. He sounds like a salamander. I just feel like slapping the food right down his throat! And that laugh is so annoying! Look at him! Yeesh! Who is this person?" Stacia said within herself in anguish. He had taken on so many demons, that he was starting to become totally unrecognizable.

"Oh, My Lord, forgive me for these evil thoughts. But this man is a stranger to me. I am so tired of his mess. Why don't you do something about him, Lord? I've been praying and believing, but he seems to be getting worse. Please help me not to lose it on him, Lord Jesus!" Stacia prayed within herself. All she could think of was all of the lies, strife, and disrespect she had endured for the last few years. "I have to do it tonight. Enough is enough!" Stacia screamed inside her mind.

As soon as Gabriel finished licking his fingers, Stacia said those fateful words that no man likes to hear. She turned the television down and said, "We need to talk!" Gabriel looked at her with wild amazement responding with frustration... "TO BE CONTINUED"!

# ALMOND EYES

## (LIFE Through Hers!)

Look for the next book to see what Stacia told Gabriel. Will she tell him that she is leaving and wants a divorce? Or will she seek to work things out? Will Gabriel explode in more disrespectful behavior? Or will he fall into line as a man of God and change his ways? Come see what Angela and Tanya are up to. And why did Mrs. Neville miss her weekly trip to the bakery at five thirty for the donut sale.

See you soon!

Prayer blog: **aiisanditisso.com**

Made in the USA
Columbia, SC
08 February 2025

52847529R00031